Why Am I Blue?

This book is dedicated to the volunteers at the Fletcher Wildlife Garden in Ottawa, Canada, who showed me the little blue frog that was living in their pond. Only one frog in a million in North America is blue.—KD

With love to my niece Julieta, my nephews Nahuel, Juan Cruz, Nazareno, and the little Juan, my new nephew of the heart.—VG

Published by
MAGINATION PRESS ®
An Educational Publishing Foundation Book
American Psychological Association
750 First Street NE
Washington, DC 20002

Magination Press is a registered trademark of the American Psychological Association.

For more information about our books, including a complete catalog, please write to us, call 1-800-374-2721, or visit our website at www.apa.org/pubs/magination.

Book design by Susan White
Printed by Worzalla, Stevens Point, WI

Library of Congress Cataloging-in-Publication Data
Names: Dakos, Kalli, author. | Garofoli, Viviana, illustrator.
Title: Why am I blue? : a story about being yourself / by Kalli Dakos ;
   illustrated by Viviana Garofoli.
Description: Washington, DC : Magination Press, [2017] | "American Psychological Association."
   | "An Educational Publishing Foundation Book."
   | Summary: The Blue Frog is unhappy and worried because he thinks he should be green like all the
   other frogs until the Very Old Frog gives an explanation.
Identifiers: LCCN 2016050781| ISBN 9781433827341 (hardcover) | ISBN 1433827344 (hardcover)
Subjects: | CYAC: Self-acceptance—Fiction. | Individuality—Fiction. | Frogs—Fiction.
Classification: LCC PZ7.D15223 Why 2017 | DDC [E]—dc23 LC record available at
   https://lccn.loc.gov/2016050781

Manufactured in the United States of America
10 9 8 7 6 5 4 3 2 1

Why Am I Blue?

A Story About
Being Yourself

by Kalli Dakos
illustrated by Viviana Garofoli

MAGINATION PRESS•WASHINGTON, DC
American Psychological Association

The Blue Frog looked
at himself in the water
and asked,
"Why am I blue?"

"I want to play, and I don't care what color you are,"
a Green Frog croaked.

"But I do care. I want to look like you and the other frogs."

"Blue is soft and warm," whispered the Sky from above. "I am blue too."

"My friends are the color of the grass,
and I want to be like them."

A Dandelion turned his head towards the frog.
"Every dandelion is yellow and turns white and fuzzy.
But I'd like to be blue and special like you."

"I don't want to be special. I want to be green."

A Leaf on the big maple tree was listening. "I was green, but in the fall I changed to red, orange, and yellow. I love my new colors."

"But you are a leaf. You are supposed to change color. I am a frog and I should be green."

A Fish poked his head out of the water. "Even if you are blue, you can still leap into the water and swim."

"I don't want to swim today. I am worried about my color."

"Worry!
Worry!
Worry!"
chirped a
freckled Bird.
"I'm not
even sure
what color I am.
But I can soar above
the trees towards the
sky and that is all
that matters."

"But when you look down from
the sky you will see one frog that
is the WRONG color."

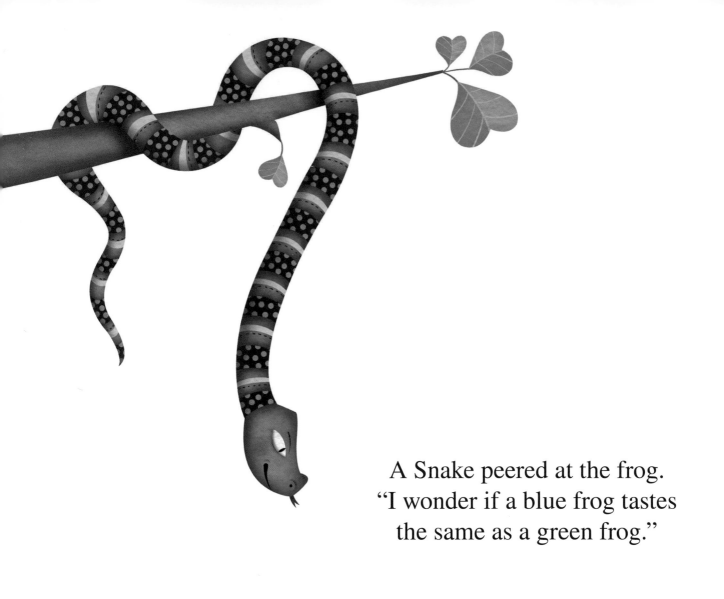

A Snake peered at the frog.
"I wonder if a blue frog tastes
the same as a green frog."

"I'd prefer that you don't eat me,
no matter what color I am."

The Very Old Frog croaked,
"I know why you are blue.
I have the answer."

"Oh, please tell me.
What is the answer?
Why am I blue?"

"You are blue because you are blue,"
said the Very Old Frog.
"And this is all you need to know."

"I am blue because I am blue?
I thought there would be a bigger answer."

"Some answers are small and they are still enough," croaked the Very Old Frog.

The Blue Frog
thought for a moment.

"I like small answers,"
he said.

"I do too," said the Green Frog.

"Come, let's dive in the pond together."

And the two frogs leapt,
as only frogs can, towards
the sky and right into
the clear water.

Note to Parents and Caregivers

by Gayle E. Pitman, PhD

All of us are different from one another in special and beautiful ways. But being different from one's peers can be hard. We all want to be part of a group, and to be accepted and loved by others. We might struggle with whether to embrace our differences, or to hide them in order to experience a sense of oneness with others. Children, especially, can face challenges with this, particularly if they experience "difference" as a form of separation, disparagement, and otherness.

How Children Experience Differences

Children notice differences at an early age. Even infants notice differences. When six-month-old babies are shown images of faces, they quickly become uninterested in looking at faces that are the same race or gender. However, when the skin color or gender changes, babies snap to attention. Clearly, babies are interested in differences, and this interest marks the beginning of their cognitive development. This is normal, and it's not necessarily a bad thing.

Once a child enters the preschool years, we see a shift in how they use differences to make decisions. Preschool-age children are hard-wired to group similar things together in order to make sense of the world. They'll sort things by various qualities, such as shape, color, or size, and group like items together. They'll begin to categorize people into groups, usually based on what's most visible, like age, gender, skin color, hair color and texture, and size. Again, this isn't a bad thing—children are merely acknowledging the realities they see in the world, and they're trying to wrap their heads around all of it. At this age, children usually accept differences without question.

Once a child reaches school age, things get a little more complicated from a developmental standpoint. First, as children are increasing their understanding of similarities, differences, and categories, they're also developing a sense of self-awareness. Second, they're starting to understand how they fit (or don't fit) into various categories. And third, they're beginning to compare themselves to their peers on the basis of these categories. All of this contributes to a child's developing value system around differences. And this is where several things can happen. Let's look at some of the possibilities.

Some differences can be a source of positive self-esteem for children. They could have qualities that are cool, quirky, and respected by others. For example, if a child is especially talented at something, like art, music, or athletics, they might feel respected by their peers, even though their talent sets them apart to some extent. Moreover, if this quality is nurtured by family members and teachers and through extracurricular activities, these differences can enhance self-esteem in a powerful way.

Differences don't always work that way, though. Some differences involve characteristics like disability, gender identity, or race, qualities that have been used throughout history to justify inequality and mistreatment. If differences aren't valued by the individual or by society, a few things can happen:

Children may want to hide or "fix" their differences. For many children, standing out from the crowd can make them feel self-conscious, particularly if their difference isn't strongly valued. In an effort to help children, adults sometimes fall into the trap of referring to children as "special." Usually this doesn't work. In *Why Am I Blue?*, the Blue Frog says, "I don't want to be special. I want to be green." Even from an early age, children understand that "specialness" doesn't always mean that they'll be accepted by others, and feel that having friends is more important than being unique.

Children may begin to develop stereotypes. As noted earlier, recognizing differences and creating categories isn't always a bad thing. However, stereotypes develop when our categories become rigid instead of flexible and fluid. Once that happens, stereotypes influence how we treat others, and how we perceive our own abilities. For example, if Alicia (who uses a wheelchair) thinks that children with physical disabilities aren't as smart as other children, that belief alone is likely to have an effect on her school performance.

Children may compare themselves to others, and use those comparisons to determine their self-worth. If a child feels "othered," that child is likely to prefer qualities that reflect the dominant group, and devalue qualities that reflect the child's own group. Here's an example: Studies of doll preferences among children show us that:

- White children, across the board, tend to prefer White dolls.
- Black children who spend most of their time with Black people tend to prefer Black dolls.
- Black children who spend most of their time with White people tend to prefer White dolls.

In other words, who you spend time with during childhood makes a big difference. In *Why Am I Blue?*, the Blue Frog says, "My friends are the color of grass, and I want to be like them." Because most of the Blue Frog's time is spent with friends who are green, the Blue Frog has started to develop a preference for green-ness.

How You Can Help

How can you help children embrace their own differences—and accept others who are different from themselves?

Acknowledge differences—and talk about them.

Talk directly with children about the very real differences that they see and experience. Don't pretend that differences don't exist, and don't send the message that they're not supposed to "see" differences. Instead, give children room to ask questions and express feelings about the differences they have, and the differences they see in others.

Recognize that children want to be accepted by their peers.

Children start to develop friendships and form peer groups as early as three or four years old. If a child is feeling rejected because they're different from their peers, acknowledge that, and allow the child to express feelings about it. That will help you determine the best way to intervene in the situation. Seek out opportunities to diversify your child's social experiences, and if your child has differences that set them apart from their peers, find ways of connecting your child with others who share these qualities. For example, find a summer camp that is specifically designed for children with disabilities, or children from particular racial and ethnic groups. Or get your child involved in an afterschool activity, like a club, sport, or class that allows your child to connect with others who share the same interests, and where participants have shared identities. There are also numerous support groups for children and families that can foster a sense of connection to and pride in one's identity.

Monitor your child's media consumption.

Numerous studies have shown that consistent exposure to media (even child-friendly media) can reinforce and amplify stereotypes. Consider limiting the amount of screen time you allow your child to have. In addition, expose your child to TV shows, movies, books, and other forms of media that depict a wide range of qualities, and that reflect your values. Doing this is good not only for reflecting your child's own differences back to them (and affirming and empowering them), but also because exposing children to depictions of people with other differences has been shown to promote empathy and reduce stereotypes. Be willing to start a conversation; if you see bias or negative attitudes towards people in the media your child consumes, point it out and talk about it.

Check your own attitudes and beliefs.

Children are very observant. They look to adults as a model for how to behave in unfamiliar situations. If you're uncomfortable around others who have certain differences, children will likely pick up on that, even if the way you express that discomfort is very subtle. You might not even be consciously aware of your bias or discomfort; we're surrounded by toxic attitudes towards certain groups of people, and it's truly impossible not to absorb some of these beliefs to some degree. Developing an ongoing practice of self-awareness is a big step towards eradicating these attitudes, and it can act as a powerful model for children. The way you handle situations that make you uncomfortable will likely determine how your child will navigate something similar in the future. Be honest with yourself about what pushes you out of your comfort zone, and be willing to work on overcoming those weak spots.

Watch your language.

Words are powerful, because the words we choose reflect how we think. One helpful approach is to use "people first" language with your children. Use words that describe the whole child, and don't focus exclusively on what makes that child different. For example, instead of referring to Nicky as "disabled," you can say that he uses crutches to move around. Instead of calling Keiko "deaf," you can describe how she uses American Sign Language interpreters to communicate with others. This puts the focus on the person, and not on any category.

Help your child understand that differences don't necessarily need to be "fixed."

Throughout this book, the Blue Frog repeatedly asks, "Why am I blue?" It's not clear why the Blue Frog is asking this question, but it's entirely possible that the Blue Frog wants to figure out how not to be blue anymore. If children have questions about what caused their differences, it can be helpful to understand why they want to know. Sometimes we know why, and sometimes we don't. In the end, the Very Old Frog tells the Blue Frog, "You are blue because you are blue. And that is all you need to know." Sometimes, knowing what caused their difference can be helpful and reassuring. And sometimes it's necessary, particularly if the difference involves a medical issue. But in many cases, knowing that their difference just is might be all they need to know. The Blue Frog is blue just because, and nothing about the Blue Frog needs to change.

Remember that some differences are easier than others.

Having a disability in a world designed for able-bodied people is hard. Being a person of color in a society that values Whiteness is hard. For a person on the autism spectrum, being expected to follow social rules set by neurotypical people is hard. Differences do make us unique. In many cases, our differences are our superpowers. But differences aren't always easy. Allow space for your child to express their feelings about that, and validate those feelings. Don't feel pressured to make these challenges go away; instead, give them room to be who they are.

These conversations aren't always easy. However, talking with your child about differences—and similarities—will go a long way towards teaching your child self-acceptance, and acceptance of others. Starting these conversations now will pay off throughout your child's life.

GAYLE E. PITMAN, PhD, is a professor of psychology and women's studies at Sacramento City College. Her teaching and writing focuses on gender and sexual orientation, and she has worked extensively with the lesbian, gay, bisexual, transgender, and queer (LGBTQ) community. She is the author of When You Look Out the Window *and* This Day In June, *which won the American Library Association's Stonewall Book Award in 2015.*

About the Author

KALLI DAKOS has been delighting readers with poetry since the release of her best-selling book, *If You're Not Here, Please Raise Your Hand.* She has written six IRA-CBC Children's Choice Selections, such as *Our Principal Promised to Kiss a Pig* and *A Funeral in the Bathroom.* A former reading specialist and frequent visitor to schools, Kalli has celebrated a love of reading and writing in schools all over Canada and the U.S. and as far away as Hong Kong. She presently resides in Ottawa, Ontario with her family and has an office in Ogdensburg, New York.

About the Illustrator

VIVIANA GAROFOLI was born in Buenos Aires, Argentina, where she currently lives with her husband, Sergio, and two daughters, April and Emma. As a child, her favorite pastime was playing with her watercolors and crayons on big sheets of paper; if asked what she wanted to be when she grew up, Viviana would immediately reply, "a painter." In 1995, she graduated from Escuela Nacional de Bellas Artes Prilidiano Pueyrredón with a degree in fine arts. Over the last 15 years, she has illustrated more than 70 children's books and contributed many editorial and textbook illustrations in Argentina and Puerto Rico. In her spare time, Viviana enjoys working in her garden, tending to her orchids.

About Magination Press

MAGINATION PRESS is an imprint of the American Psychological Association, the largest scientific and professional organization representing psychologists in the United States and the largest association of psychologists worldwide.